Dawson's Creek

The Official Scrapbook

BASED ON THE TELEVISION SHOW
DAWSON'S CREEK
CREATED BY KEVIN WILLIAMSON

BY K.S. RODRIGUEZ

POCKET BOOKS
New York   London   Toronto   Sydney   Tokyo   Singapore

An *Original* Publication of POCKET BOOKS
POCKET BOOKS, a division of Simon and Schuster Inc.
1230 Avenue of the Americas, New York, NY 10020

Interior Book Design by Mark Pessoni

Childhood photos of Joshua Jackson on pages 22 and 23 copyright and courtesy of Joshua Jackson

ISBN: 0-671-02673-9

First Pocket Books printing November 1998
10 9 8 7 6 5 4 3
POCKET and colophon are registered trademarks of Simon & Schuster Inc.

DAWSON'S CREEK is a registered trademark of Columbia TriStar Television, Inc.

Printed in the U.S.A.

SOMETIMES BEING A WRITER CAN GET YOU INTO TROUBLE.

For example, imagine writing about something completely autobiographical like *Dawson's Creek*. Then imagine actually *admitting* that it's autobiographical. Your friends laugh at you. Critics pulverize you. And your mom and dad just want to know how come they never knew about your unconditional love for Katie Couric.

It's certainly no secret that I borrow a lot of my own personal history when I write. For example, *Dawson's Creek* is a little inlet of water near a bridge just about five miles from where I grew up. Joey is based on my high school sweetheart, Fanny Norwood. She's the one I pined for, secretly, and agonizingly watched as she dated all the hot high school studs. Fortunately, when they finally broke her heart (which they always did) I was there to help her pick up the pieces.

Dawson Leery's love for Spielberg definitely doesn't come out of nowhere. I believe Spielberg to be god and the primary influence in my professional life. I read once that he made home movies in his backyard, so I found an old 8mm camera that my parents had packed away and shot my own home movies. My first, WHITE AS A GHOST, included a cherry Jell-O decapitation sequence complete with spaghetti noodles.

Dawson's Creek is my true love. It combines all the memories of my childhood (and a lot of memories the writers and I created to make it more exciting—because *nobody's* life is that exciting) with the kind of storytelling that I always hope to be a part of. Part real, part Hollywood fantasy. My work is both. My goal is to take smart and articulate characters who can comment, poke fun, agonize, be surprised, laugh at themselves, self-referentiate, but ultimately react very honestly and humanly to what's happening around them.

Of course, this show isn't all my doing—not even close. There is a huge group of incredibly talented, dedicated people that bring this show to life week after week. The cast: James, Josh, Michelle, Katie, John, Mary-Margaret, Nina, and Mary Beth. They are all wonderfully gifted actors and delightful human beings. And the writing team, who have managed to take my dream and turn it into such a tremendous reality. The show is theirs. And the joyous and fearless leader everyone has in Paul Stupin, the other Executive Producer and my co-conspirator/partner in crime. Without this group, *Dawson's Creek* would not be. (And it doesn't hurt to be involved with the heroes at Columbia/TriStar TV and the WB Network, either.)

We couldn't be more thrilled that *Dawson's Creek* has reached its audience with the kind of emotional force that we only ever dreamed about. Kids, fathers, boyfriends, college students, grandmothers, high school freshmen—everyone has tuned in week after week to experience the world of Dawson, Joey, Pacey, and Jen. To laugh with them or cry with them. To share in the stories that they live through. To know them, as we all do. And we plan to continue their journey for as long as we can, because it would be a shame to miss out on any of it.

Kevin Williamson

It has the perfect mix for must-watch television: juicy plots, romantic tension, quick-as-a-whip dialogue, and smart, articulate, authentic characters. The high-quality scripts combined with skilled acting and the magic of a small, charming town make *Dawson's Creek* unique. But there are four other elements that have fans absolutely wild over the show: James Van Der Beek (Dawson), Katie Holmes (Joey), Joshua Jackson (Pacey), and Michelle Williams (Jen). These young talents perfectly capture teenage passion, insecurity, and angst to turn out genuine performances that have been wowing critics and fans the world over.

What are James, Josh, Katie, and Michelle really like? What did these young actors do before they landed in Capeside? Which star is most like his or her character? Who likes to dance in the makeup trailer? Which actor brings a dog to the set each day? And what other projects can fans look forward to seeing them in? Turn the page and find out . . . .

Did you know? On the set, the actors sit in chairs with their characters' names on them—not their own names— to lessen the likelihood of fans stealing the canvas backs.

awson Leery, age fifteen, is the only child of Mitch and Gale Leery. His life revolves around film: he takes a film class at Capeside High; he and best pal, Joey, spend every Friday night—"movie night"—watching movie after movie; he works part-time in Capeside's video store; and he spends most of his spare time making his own films. His dream is to follow in the footsteps of his idol, filmmaker Steven Spielberg.

Because of his avid interest in film, Dawson is a dreamer and tends to romanticize life. He wishes his life were more like the movies, but he does have two feet on the ground. Dawson is smart and sensitive, an attentive boyfriend who likes to surprise his girl with sweet romantic gestures, and a good friend who's always there to lend a sympathetic ear.

Though he fell for Jen Lindley when she first came to town, his feelings for his best friend, Joey Potter, have been heating up. Dawson finds himself caught in a confusing love triangle that allures and scares him at the same time.

As a child, Dawson was short and pudgy, which earned him the nickname "Oompa-Loompa," after the diminutive people in *Willy Wonka and the Chocolate Factory.* But in his teens, he has far outgrown his nickname by emerging into a tall, slender, handsome, clean-cut teenager with the makings of an out-and-out heartthrob. Just ask Joey . . . .

"I believe that all the mysteries of the universe, all the answers to all life's questions, can be found in a Spielberg film. It's a theory I've been working on. See, whenever I have a problem, all I have to do is look to the right Spielberg movie and the answer is revealed."—Dawson Leery

Did you know? After several unsuccessful attempts at molding a latex "Joey" face for Dawson's famous mask-kissing scene, the props people came up with something else. The "rubber" Joey mask on which Dawson practiced his kissing technique was actually concrete—and weighed about 30 pounds!

JAMES VAN DER BEEK

James Van Der Beek, the oldest of three children, was born in Cheshire, Connecticut. He was bitten by the acting bug literally by accident, after a concussion at age thirteen landed him off the football field and into the theater as Danny Zuko in *Grease*. When James' parents saw the talent their son had, they allowed him to start auditioning for jobs in New York City at the age of sixteen.

Before long, he won roles in an off-Broadway play, Edward Albee's *Finding the Sun* and in *Shenandoah* at the Goodspeed Opera House in Connecticut. He snagged his first film role soon after, as an arrogant jock in *Angus*—a far cry from sensitive Dawson.

James claims he is like Dawson: "He's a lot like I was at fifteen—innocent, idealistic, impassioned, and often clueless." He thinks viewers relate to Dawson because he is "the dork in all of us."

But James was no Oompa-Loompa as a kid. He earned the nickname "Beek" on the football team, stemming from his Dutch last name, which means "by the brook." But the nickname that stuck was "Baby James," which cast members in a play called him to distinguish him from four older Jameses in the production.

After winning a scholarship to Drew University, James put his career on hold for his education. He enjoyed studying English and Sociology at the Madison, New Jersey, school, but he soon missed being on stage and in front of the camera. Restless, he searched out more work and came upon the lead role in *Dawson's Creek*. The script impressed him: he wanted that role.

Meanwhile, the producers of *Dawson's Creek* felt they had exhausted their search, and as time was coming close for the series to be filmed, they didn't know if they'd ever find the right lead. But James's audition tape caught the attention of the casting

Full name: James William Van Der Beek
Nickname: Baby James, Beek
Birth Date: March 8, 1977
Star Sign: Pisces
Birthplace: Cheshire, Connecticut
Siblings: One younger brother and one younger sister
Hobbies: Sports, reading, writing, shooting pool
Favorite Color: Blue

directors, and it was immediately FedExed to producer Paul Stupin's home. Stupin watched the tape and sighed with relief: he had finally found Dawson. Three days later, James was notified that he had won the role. James certainly left an impression, his audition tape became stuck in Stupin's VCR. It is still stuck there to this day.

James plans to return to school eventually, but right now he is riding a rocket to superstardom with the busy *Dawson's Creek* filming schedule and two movies ready for release: he costars in *I Love You. . . I Love You Not* with teen sensation Claire Danes, and in an independent film, *Harvest*.

When James is off-screen, he enjoys boating with *Dawson's Creek's* cast and crew, reading favorite books such as James Joyce's *Portrait of the Artist as a Young Man*, writing, and playing sports.

Did you know? It takes seven full days of shooting to make one episode of *Dawson's Creek*.

This new girl in town turned many heads in Capeside when she arrived, especially Dawson Leery's. Jen arrived in town just in time to start her sophomore year at Capeside High School. Her parents sent her to live in the small town ostensibly to help care for her ill grandfather but really to get away from the big-city temptations, bad influences, and ex-boyfriends that New York City had to offer. Instead of life in the fast lane, she has taken a few steps back to grow up in quiet Capeside—and in the process even learned a thing or two.

Grappling with religious Grams isn't easy for Jen, and experiencing her grandfather's slow death was harder than she ever imagined. And even though not everyone in Capeside was as friendly as Dawson and Cliff Elliot, she eventually found her niche, and a friend in her chief rival, Joey Potter.

Jen is mature, thoughtful, self-confident, intellectual, and sophisticated without being snobby, and she just wants to lead the life of a normal teenage girl. Despite her past, she seems to have her head on straight, but she does experience moments of uncertainty and insecurity, though she tries her best not to let it show.

"You know, I really am a cliché, Dawson. In New York I was moving fast. I was moving really, really fast. I kept stumbling and falling. But here I feel like for the first time in a long time, I'm walking at a steady pace. And I'm afraid that if I kiss you my knees may buckle, I may stumble, and I don't think I could deal with that right now."—Jen Lindley

Did you know? Unlike Jen and Joey, Michelle and Katie instantly bonded in real life.

MICHELLE WILLIAMS

Born in Kalispell, Montana, Michelle Williams made a change from small town life to the big city when her family moved to San Diego when she was ten years old—just the opposite of her character, Jen Lindley. In San Diego, Michelle became involved in community theater and then started to commute to Los Angeles to audition for television and movie roles. She soon won guest appearances on television shows such as *Step by Step* and *Home Improvement*, then landed her first feature film role at the age of fourteen in *Lassie*, followed quickly by the role of an alien in the sci-fi cult hit *Species*. When more parts started to come in, Michelle accelerated her high school classes, graduated early at the age of 16, and continued to work in film. One of her greatest learning experiences was acting beside movie greats Jessica Lange, Jennifer Jason Leigh, and Michelle Pfeiffer in *A Thousand Acres*.

When Michelle auditioned for the role of Jen, the producers thought she brought the perfect blend of maturity, rebelliousness, and vulnerability to the role with her great acting and stunning good looks. Michelle is mature and introspective like Jen, and she can relate to Jen's plight of feeling like an outsider in Capeside: Michelle told one teen magazine that she spent most of her time in high school hiding in the bathroom stalls from bullies.

In her free time, Michelle is a voracious reader who enjoys watching 1980s teen flicks with Katie Holmes and keeping fit by running and boxing. Fans can look forward to seeing Michelle in the films *Halloween H20*, starring Jamie Lee Curtis and written by Kevin Williamson, and *Dick*, with Kirsten Dunst, about two girls who get lost on a White House tour and meet President Richard Nixon.

Did you know? Michelle's girlhood dream was to become the first female heavyweight champion of the world.

Full Name:	Michelle Williams	Birthplace:	Kalispell, Montana
Nickname:	None	Siblings:	Four
Birth Date:	September 9, 1980	Hobbies:	Reading, boxing
Star Sign:	Virgo		

Trouble. Incompetent. An embarrassment. That's how Pacey Witter's intolerant family would characterize him. But his best friends would call him sensitive, independent, eager, insecure, witty, and disarmingly charming. Pacey is the youngest in his hard-core family of three older sisters and one older brother. His father is Capeside's sheriff, putting a lot of pressure on him to behave, not to mention his brother, Doug, dutiful deputy to Dad and chronic Pacey-harasser. Like Joey, he uses his sense of humor and sharp wit as a guard to his sensitive soul: deep down, Pacey wants to be liked and accepted. And though it may not seem like it at first, Pacey does try to do the right thing.

Pacey has had bad luck with girls his age, which might explain why he was drawn to his English teacher, Tamara Jacobs. His brief time with her taught him a lot of painful but valuable lessons, and he surprisingly handled the scandal and breakup with the grace of a mature man.

An underachiever, he's not a student, though he is smart. Pacey doesn't see why he should rise above everyone's (low) expectations of him. Though he's not a jock, he enjoys sports, especially basketball. He earns extra money by working at Screenplay Video with his best buddy, Dawson. There's never a dull moment with Pacey, whether it is because of his offbeat sense of humor or his unabashed antics, like "borrowing" his father's car or entering a beauty pageant.

"You know what Dawson? I don't know how to tell you this—but the guy with the brown hair and the throbbing neck muscles . . . the guy with Tamara Jacobs . . . that's . . . that's . . . me."—Pacey Witter

Did you know? In the "Detention" episode Pacey (the character) refers to *The Mighty Ducks* movies that Josh (the actor) starred in.

JOSHUA "JOSH" JACKSON

Though he's only in his early twenties, Josh Jackson already had a truckload of acting experience behind him when he joined the cast of *Dawson's Creek*. His career started in his hometown of Vancouver, Canada, where he appeared in television ads promoting tourism in British Columbia. By the age of eleven he had already won a role in a feature film, *Crooked Hearts*, and soon thereafter landed the lead in the Seattle production of *Willy Wonka and the Chocolate Factory*. His biggest break came with the Disney hit *The Mighty Ducks*, which went on to have two sequels in which Josh co-starred. Other movie parts quickly followed, in *Andre the Seal*, *Digger*, and *Magic in the Water*. Joshua also starred in two Showtime films, *Robin of Locksley* and *Ronnie and Julie*.

When the producers of *Dawson's Creek* saw Josh's audition for Pacey, they knew

they had found their man. They felt that Josh perfectly captured Pacey's sly attitude. Soon they found out that was for a reason—cast and crew agree that Josh is most like his character. "Like Pacey, I also have an offbeat sense of humor and I enjoy laughing, having a good time, and often get myself in trouble for it. But neither of us is mischievous for mischief's sake. Pacey's in his own world, doing his own thing, which unfortunately seems to offend a lot of people." Despite the similarities, Josh seems to be slightly more serious than Pacey: though he's the clown on the set, Josh also enjoys reading philosophy.

Off the set, Josh enjoys spending time with the cast and crew of *Dawson's Creek*, who in turn say he is "fun to hang with," and his constant companion, Shumba, a large Rhodesian Ridgeback, who loyally comes to work with Josh every day.

Fans can look forward to seeing Josh in more feature films, including *Apt Pupil*, a film based on a Stephen King short story in which he co-stars with Brad Renfro, and *Urban Legend*, a spin on the horror film genre, co-starring with Jared Leto and Alicia Witt, and *Cruel Inventions*, a modern version of *Dangerous Liaisons*, set in an affluent prep school, starring Ryan Phillipe and Sarah Michelle Geller.

Full Name: Joshua Jackson
Nickname: Josh, Jackson
Birth Date: June 11, 1978
Star Sign: Gemini
Birthplace: Vancouver, British Columbia
Favorite Color: Brown
Pets: Shumba, a Rhodesian Ridgeback
Siblings: One younger sister
Hobbies: Reading, sports

Left, above, and right: Cute from the start! Josh's own family photos capture his star personality.

There's more than meets the eye to this fifteen-year-old girl next door—or rather, girl across the creek. Tomboy Josephine "Joey" Potter has had to grow up quickly, learning the hard way to be self-reliant. Having lost her mother to cancer, and with her father in prison, Joey lives with her older sister, Bessie, and Bessie's infant son, Alexander. Joey and her makeshift family struggle but are able to make ends meet through the S. S. Icehouse, the touristy restaurant Bessie runs, where Joey waits on tables. Though Joey's family situation fuels small–town gossip in Capeside, Joey is able to rise above it all and wade through her difficult teenage years with hopes of getting a college scholarship.

Joey comes across as tough and self-assured, with a sharp tongue and intelligence, but inside she's insecure about her budding beauty and sexuality. Her feelings about best pal Dawson have especially confused her: they quickly changed from companionship to longing. When Jen Lindley comes into the picture and steals Dawson's heart, these feelings plague Joey even more, and she eventually gets what she wants. Things start to ignite between her and Dawson, leaving her utterly bewildered. Joey wonders if their relationship can stand the heat. . . .

"I just think our emerging hormones are destined to alter our relationship and I'm trying to limit the fallout."—Joey Potter

KATIE HOLMES

Katie Holmes was born in Toledo, Ohio, the youngest of five children. Though Katie had Tinseltown aspirations, she never thought she'd be able to break out of her small-town life and burst onto the entertainment scene so quickly.

In Toledo, Katie studied at a modeling school and acted in high school productions. When an agent spotted her at a modeling convention and encouraged her to come to Los Angeles, she nervously accepted the offer. She found herself at her first professional audition ever, for the critically acclaimed and award winning film, *The Ice Storm*, starring Kevin Kline and Sigourney Weaver. Katie's sparkling talent won her the role in an instant.

That gave Katie the courage to audition for *Dawson's Creek*. Her mother taped her audition in the basement of their house. Producers of *Dawson's Creek* didn't care much about the quality of Katie's tape, but they did care a great deal about Katie's acting talent. They immediately knew they had found their Joey in sweet, small-town girl Katie Holmes.

When *Dawson's Creek* producers contacted Katie for a callback, she had a major problem: they wanted her to come out to Los Angeles just when she was set to star in her high school production of *Damn Yankees*. Rather than back out on her responsibility to her school, Katie asked the producers to postpone her callback until after the musical ended its run.

Co–stars and producers can't believe that sweet, beautiful, naive Katie is playing a tomboy with an acid tongue. And unlike Joey, she's isn't very good at rowing a boat—the boat is actually towed by an underwater rope. But Katie does think she has a few things in common with her

character. She told *Us* magazine, "I'm actually working on becoming more like my character. She's so smart and strong. And witty."

Katie's fans have a lot to look forward to in the next couple of years in addition to *Dawson's Creek*. Her film projects include *Disturbing Behavior*, in which she plays a character a lot less wholesome than Joey Potter; *Killing Mrs. Tingle*, another Kevin Williamson vehicle; and *Go*, in which she stars with *Party of Five* heartthrob Scott Wolf.

Full Name: Katherine Holmes
Nickname: Katie
Birth Date: December 18, 1978
Star Sign: Sagittarius
Birthplace: Toledo, Ohio
Siblings: Three older sisters and one older brother
Hobbies: Dancing and shopping

LOCATION, LOCATION, LOCATION

The interior of Dawson's room is a studio set, but the exterior of the Leery house is a private home near Hewletts Creek, North Carolina.

Though Capeside is supposed to be a waterside hamlet in New England, it is in reality a picturesque seaside town in Wilmington, North Carolina.

When Dawson and Pacey aren't in school, they earn extra cash at Screenplay Video. The interior of Capeside High is shot in an old studio that was used for the show *Matlock*. Exterior scenes are filmed at the University of North Carolina at Wilmington.

Did you know? The producers vowed to try to shoot all water scenes in the summer after Katie and Josh nearly froze during the November shoot of their snail-gathering scene.

Being a native of North Carolina, creator-producer-writer Kevin Williamson chose the state for the settings of both *I Know What You Did Last Summer* and *Dawson's Creek*. He loves the beauty and the familiarity of the area. Wilmington has a big screen and small screen history, having been the backdrop for films such as *Firestarter*, *To Gillian on Her 37th Birthday*, *The Hudsucker Proxy*, *Lolita* and *Billy Bathgate* and for television shows such as *American Gothic* and *Matlock*.

Michelle, James, Katie, and Josh relax between takes. The stars are friends off the set, too. At one point, Josh and James shared an apartment in Wilmington, and the four of them enjoy hanging with the crew at Vinnie's and the Deluxe, their favorite local eateries.

SCENES WE'D LIKE TO SEE AGAIN... AND AGAIN

New Girl in Town: There's a new girl in Capeside, and while Pacey and Dawson are eager to meet and greet . . .

. . . Joey is a little less enthusiastic . . .

. . . especially when Jen is chosen to star with her in Dawson's movie.

Life Is a Carnival: It's a double date with Dawson and Mary Beth and Cliff and Jen. But who likes whom?

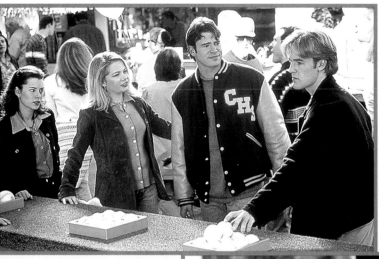

While Dawson and Cliff vie for Jen's attention, Mary Beth hopes Cliff will broaden his horizons and notice her.

Who can blame both girls if they choose their stuffed animals over the boys and their puffed-up egos?

Pageantry: The Miss Windjammer Contest brought many things to light:

. . . Joey can sing, Pacey looks smashing in a tuxedo (and should have won the contest) . . .

. . . and when Dawson stops looking through the camera and starts looking at real life, he finally realizes that his best friend Joey is a babe!

A Kiss Is Just a Kiss—or Is It?: The beginning of the end for Dawson and Jen signals a new beginning for best buddies Dawson and Joey. Dawson and Joey strive to answer the question: can best friends be lovers?

STYLES OF THE STARS

The look in Capeside is casual cool, and each character has a unique style that signals exactly who he or she is. Joey's sexy-casual halter and shorts accentuate her tomboy femininity. Dawson is comfortable in a T-shirt and baggy shorts. His pendant makes an earthy and offbeat statement.

Individualist Pacey sports a retro-cool style, shown in his penchant for bowling shirts. Jen easily makes the transition from urban chic to Capeside comfort in this breezy floral dress. Her flip-do brings out the voguish city girl at heart.

Joey's classic straight locks extend her simple charm, whether she wears her hair loose, or up in a twist. Even though Joey characterizes Pacey as "a D student with a Julius Caesar haircut," he's right in style. Dawson's locks are more poetic, a nice loose contrast to his usual neat flannel shirts and khakis.

There's nothing mismatched about Dawson and Joey.

CONTINUED:

                    JOEY
        We're fifteen, we start high school on
        Monday....and I have breasts.

                    DAWSON
        ~~WHAT?~~ 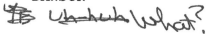 Uh-huh. What?

                    JOEY
        And you have genitalia.

                    DAWSON
        I've always had genitalia.

                    JOEY
        But there's more of it.

                    DAWSON
        How do you know?

                    JOEY
            (matter of fact)
        Long fingers--gotta go. Seeya.

Joey starts to crawl out the window.

                    DAWSON
        Whoah Joe. Don't hit and run, explain
        yourself.

                    JOEY
        We're not kids anymore. It's time to
        evolvvvvve.

                    DAWSON
        Wait a second. Has something happened
        you're not telling me?

                    JOEY
        ~~Nothing notable~~. I just think our
        emerging hormones are destined to alter
        our relationship ~~and I'm trying to limit
        the fallout~~.

                    DAWSON
        ~~What fallout? Are you saying we can't be
        friends anymore?~~

                    JOEY
        ~~I'm saying we're changing~~ and we have to
        adjust or the male-female thing will get
        in the way.

These two teleplay pages from the pilot episode show hand-written comments and changes from creator-writer-producer Kevin Williamson. His knack for writing smart teen dialogue makes *Dawson's Creek* distinctive. The actors often say that his lines roll off the tongue, making their acting job easy.

                                        (CONTINUED)

CONTINUED:

                    JEN
          Well...that depends on a lot of things.
          Gramps' heart condition, my mom and
          dad...

Jen, eyeing Joey, changes the subject.

                    JEN
          I love your lipstick. What shade is
          that?

Dawson takes note. Joey is stung with embarrassment. She
rebounds instantly.

                    JOEY
          Wicked red. Look, guys, let's just jump
          to the chase here 'cause this sweaty palm
          foreplay is getting old real quick. Jen,
          are you a virgin?

[handwritten: I like your hair colors; what # is that? Return w/ hair line]

Jen chokes on air. Dawson's mouth drops.

                    DAWSON
          That's mature.

                    JOEY
          Because Dawson is a virgin and two
          virgins really makes for a clumsy first
          encounter. Don't you think?

                    DAWSON
          You are gonna die. Painfully.

                    JOEY
          I'm just trying to escalate the process.
          Some of us are falling asleep here.

                    JEN
          It's okay, Dawson. Yes, I'm a virgin.
          How about you Joey, are you?

She smiles, challenging Joey.

                    JOEY
          Please. Years ago. Trucker named Bubba.

[handwritten: go inside. See something that fries up Joey. comes out of nowhere. out born in barn]

Jen is making a genuine effort. Dawson leans into Joey's
ear.

                    DAWSON
          What is up with you?

Joey shrugs as they move to the ticket window.

DID YOU KNOW?

Did you know? James' father pitched for the Los Angeles Dodgers.

Did you know? Because school was in session during the filming of the "Detention" episode and the producers wanted to use the local high school library, the episode had to be filmed after school hours, from 5:00 P.M. until about 5:00 A.M.

Did you know? Katie had to sit still for about two hours—three different times—while rubber was poured on her face to make the "Joey mask" on which Dawson practices his kissing.

Did you know? Josh once sang with the San Francisco Boys Chorus.

Did you know? Katie has been accepted at Columbia University, an Ivy League school in New York City. She has deferred admission.

Did you know? Josh received two marriage proposals from Japanese fans after *The Mighty Ducks* movies came out.

Did you know? The worst thing about filming by the creek is the bugs!

Did you know? *Dawson's Creek* is becoming the most talked about show on the air. It is also the WB network's highest rated show ever.

"A thang? No, I'm not getting a thang for you, Dawson. I've known you too long. I've seen you burp, barf, pick your nose, scratch your butt. I don't think I'm getting a thang for you."—Joey

Jen: Hey Joey, I love your lipstick. What shade is that?
Joey: Wicked red. I love your hair color. What number is that?

Pacey: Come on, Jen. I mean, it's pretty obvious that you're missing the undivided attention of our friend Dawson. Maybe feeling a little dumper's remorse?
Jen: You're way off.
Pacey: Tell me, is it the possibility of losing him to somebody that suddenly makes him seem attractive?
Jen: You really think I'm that shallow, huh?
Pacey: No, I think you're that human.

Joey: No time to talk, Dawson. My sister's having her baby.
Dawson: Cool. Congratulations.
Joey: On your lawn.

"That's right. I'm done trying to turn my life into some exciting movie because you know what? I'll only end up getting disappointed. Like when I started seeing Jen—I thought, okay, you know what—from now on everything is gonna be some big epic romance—you know, tortured and passionate and romantic—some big happy ending. It wasn't like that at all. The characters were flawed and uninspired. The love scenes were amateurish, to say the least. And the ending was definitely not happy. It wasn't even tragic. It just ended."—Dawson

"Dawson, fasten your seat belt. It's going to be a bumpy life."—Joey

"Unrequited love makes you do strange things . . . I mean . . . you know . . . so I've heard."—Joey

Jen: Actually, I kind of made plans with Cliff tonight. I can't come.
Dawson: Oh, really?
Jen: Does that bother you?
Dawson: Should it?
Jen: I don't know.
Dawson: Does it bother you that it doesn't bother me?
Jen: Should it?
Dawson: I don't know.
Jen: No, no it doesn't bother me.
Joey: Well, I'm glad nobody's bothered.

Pacey: Dr. Rand, I'd like to lodge a formal protest. You never told me I'd be working with a repressed control freak.
Joey: Yeah, and you never told me my grade is dependent upon some remedial underachiever.
Dr. Rand: Well, wonderful. So I see no introductions are necessary.

Mysterious voice on the phone: So tell me your name.
Jen: Drew Barrymore. Look, you wanna play this game, let's cut right to the chase. What's your favorite scary movie?
Voice: *Friday the 13th.* What's yours?
Jen: *The Ten Commandments.* Don't ask.

Jen: You know, now that the proverbial wedge we so fondly refer to as Dawson Leery is no longer between us, we could actually be friends...I know, I know, it's a bizarre concept, but we might find that we have something more in common than just the boy next door.
Joey: We don't have to, like, wash each other's hair and do each other's nails, do we?

Pacey: I'm the drummer for Pearl Jam. You?
Girl: You're dumber than who?

Pacey: Please don't make me eat dinner with the Stepford family.
Joey: Uh oh, touble in paradise? I guess I can scrape something up. I think I saw some rat droppings behind the oven.
Pacey: Great. I'll take 'em. Toss 'em in the microwave, warm 'em up, you know . . . .
Joey: That was weird. For a second there, I was overcome with this wave of sympathy for you . . . . it'll pass.

Dawson: I just want to let you know that I completely understand the absurdity of this moment. I actually thought of sending over a drink or saying something clever . . . what's your sign? I figured directness would be the best approach—i.e. "My name is Dawson." Not that my name in and of itself should impress you, but kind of in the hopes that you might, in response, tell me your name.
Nina: Did it occur to you that maybe I'm just not interested?
Dawson: No, but blind optimism is one of my faults.
Nina: One of your faults? Do you have many?
Dawson: Let's see. There's my reckless disregard for danger. My tiresome romanticism. And then of course, there's the way that I keep talking long after the person I'm trying to impress has lost all interest.

Joey: [*The English Patient*] is the only thing that's put the baby to sleep. Because the baby never sleeps. And if the baby doesn't sleep then I don't sleep. And if I don't sleep, I get angry. I get irritable. And I no longer maintain my sunny disposition. So, Pacey, if you have even the slightest bit of human decency you'll rent this movie to me immediately and bring one hundred and eighty-one minutes of peace in my otherwise wretched life. Please?
Pacey: Alright, but in my professional opinion, you don't need a video store, you need a pharmacy.

Dawson: Joe, let's assess. What have we learned from tonight's 90210 evening?
Joey: That we should always stay home on a Saturday night and watch movies because the rewind on the remote of life does not work.

Billy: So this is really it? You are leaving me for a guy who has an E.T. doll on his bed.
Jen: It's a collector's item.
Billy: It is a doll.

Bessie: He's still our father.
Joey: Yeah. Our father who art in prison.

"She's . . . great. I mean, she's . . . she's smart, she's beautiful, she's funny. She's a big old scaredy-cat. If you creep up from behind her, she'll jump out of her skin. It's pretty amusing. She's honest—she calls them just like she sees them. You can always count on getting the truth from Joey, even if the truth hurts. She's stubborn—we fight a lot. She can be so frustrating sometimes. But she's a really, really good friend. And loyal to a fault . . . she believes in me. And I'm a dreamer, so I mean it's good to have someone like that in my life. If she goes away, I don't know what I'm gonna do . . . I mean she's . . . she's my best friend. She's more than that. But . . . she's everything."—Dawson

"It's all about romance . . . and Chap Stick."—Mr. Leery

"You're the sea creature from your own movie."—Joey to Dawson

Dawson: When you broke up with me, among the many questions I asked you was "Why?" Do you remember that? And do you remember your response? Your very convincing, very heartfelt response? That you needed to be alone. That there were too many men in your life, and you needed time away from those men. And correct me if I'm wrong, Jen, but Cliff Elliot isn't exactly with the women's auxiliary.
Jen: He's a date, alright? It's not like I'm planning an engagement party.

KEEP IN TOUCH

The best way to visit Capeside is through Dawson's Desktop—available only at the official *Dawson's Creek* web site at www.dawsonscreek.com. Meet other *Dawson's Creek* fans, create your own home page, read Dawson's journal and e-mails, play games and hang out with Dawson and the gang in Capeside.